a little polar bear story

Lars' Storybook Adventure

Adaptation by Scott Peterson

Illustrations by DiCicco Studios

Sterling Publishing Co., Inc.
New York

Library of Congress Cataloging-in-Publication Data Available

2 4 6 8 10 9 7 5 3 1

Published by Sterling Publishing Co., Inc.
387 Park Avenue South, New York, NY 10016
Text copyright © 2001 by Nord-Süd Verlag AG, Gossau Zürich, Switzerland
Illustrations copyright © 2003 by Nord-Süd Verlag AG
First published in Switzerland under the title *Der kleine Eisbär rettet seine Freunde*
English translation copyright © 2003 by Night Sky Books,
a division of North-South Books Inc., New York
Distributed in Canada by Sterling Publishing
C/o Canadian Manda Group, One Atlantic Avenue, Suite 105
Toronto, Ontario, Canada M6K 3E7
Distributed in Great Britain and Europe by Chris Lloyd at Orca Book
Services, Stanley House, Fleets Lane, Poole BH15 3AJ, England
Distributed in Australia by Capricorn Link (Australia) Pty. Ltd.
P.O. Box 704, Windsor, NSW 2756, Australia

Sterling ISBN 1-4027-1279-0

Once upon a time, a little polar bear named Lars lived with his mother and father in the land of ice and snow.

Lars's best friend in the whole world was Robby the seal.

Robby had saved Lars from drowning once, and after that the
two of them played together every day.

Lars and Robby loved to run and slide and have snowball fights. Lars's parents were amazed—they'd never heard of a polar bear and a seal being friends. Polar bears and seals were supposed to be enemies.

One day, Lars and Robby noticed three big polar bears sneaking up on a group of seals.

"Hey!" Lars called out to the seals. "Watch out!"

At the sound of Lars's voice, the seals looked up and saw the hungry polar bears heading toward them. Quickly, they jumped into the water and swam away as fast as they could.

That night, the three angry polar bears met with Lars's father, Mika.

"It's bad enough that your son is friends with a seal," Brutus growled. "But now he's making it so we can't even eat!"

Sophocles the walrus had to agree. "I'm afraid you're going to have to put an end to their friendship, Mika."

"My father says we can't be friends anymore," Lars said sadly.
"I know," said Robby. "Mine said the same thing."
"Well . . . good-bye, Robby." Lars tried not to cry.
"Bye, Lars," said Robby.

Lars sadly watched his friend leave.

"Wait!" he cried. "I have an idea!" He quickly told Robby
his plan.

The next day on the ice floe Lars explained his idea to the seals and polar bears. "You said Robby and I can't be friends— because polar bears eat seals, right?"

Everyone nodded.

Lars smiled. "Well, polar bears eat fish, too. And seals are great at catching fish. What if we asked the seals for help? I'm sure they would catch extra fish for us—as long as we promised not to eat any more of them. Then everyone will have enough to eat!"

Lars's plan was perfect.

From that day on, the polar bears and the seals got along just fine.

Everyone was happy.

Until the day there were no more fish.

"I don't know what happened, but all the fish are gone!" said a seal.

"I bet the humans took them all," a polar bear grumbled.

But no one knew what to do.

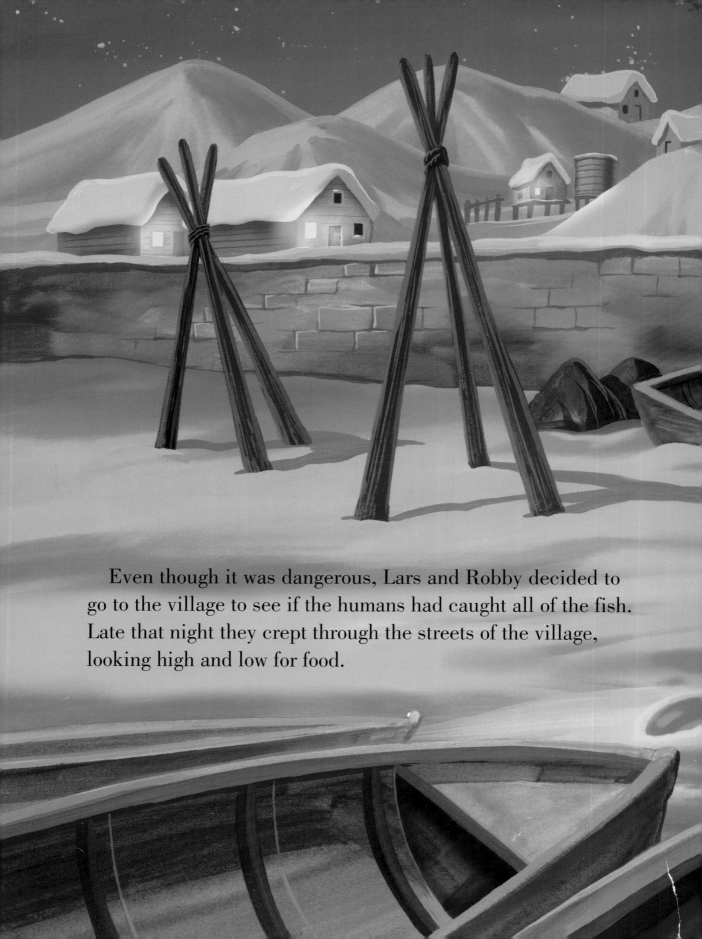

Even though it was dangerous, Lars and Robby decided to go to the village to see if the humans had caught all of the fish. Late that night they crept through the streets of the village, looking high and low for food.

Suddenly a dog jumped out at Lars and began to chase him. Lars dashed into a small house to hide.

"Hello," said a soft voice. "What do we have here?" Lars looked up and saw a little girl peering in at him.

"I'm Lena," she said. "You look hungry." She held out
a fish stick. "Everyone in the village is hungry, too. A
ship with a black mouth has been taking away all of the
fish. All I can give you are some leftover fish sticks."

Lars gobbled up the leftovers.

When Lars got home, he tried to tell the others about the black ship . . . but he was too late.

Suddenly the ice and snow exploded. All the animals were
thrown into the icy water as a big, black mouth came crashing
through the ice.

The black mouth swallowed up everything in its path—seals, fish, and polar bears.

Lars had escaped but he'd never been so scared in his life. He knew he had to help. He knew he had to save his friends.

Gathering up all of his courage, Lars swam right up to the ship and made it chase him. The ship was huge. And fast. Lars led the ship toward a big iceberg.

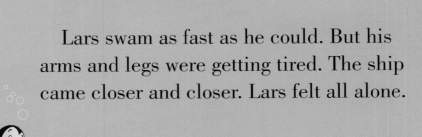

Lars swam as fast as he could. But his arms and legs were getting tired. The ship came closer and closer. Lars felt all alone.

Lars didn't realize it, but his friends Greta and Caruso were right behind him, trying to save the others, too. Greta grabbed Lars just as the black mouth was about to trap him inside and helped him swim away. They were just in time.

Crash! The ship smashed into the iceberg, and sank.

The mouth of the ship opened just wide enough for the animals to escape. They jumped out and swam as fast as they could away from the ship.

"Hooray!" a seal shouted. "Now all the fish will come back!"
Everyone was celebrating.
Especially Lars and Robby—best friends forever.